lassic

Modern English

Snow White and The Seven Dwarfs

Adapted and Annotated
by
Mohamed Brahim

Foreword

Snow White, a kind and beautiful princess lived with her stepmother, the queen.

This stepmother was evil, vain and wicked. Every day she would stand in front of her magic mirror and say, "Mirror, mirror on the wall, who is the most beautiful one of all?"

The mirror always answered that the queen was the most beautiful of all. But one day it answered that Snow White was the most beautiful one of all. The jealous queen ordered a huntsman to take Snow White to the forest to have her killed. The huntsman, feeling sorry for the poor princess, abandoned her in the forest and brought back a wild boar's heart to prove to the queen that he had murdered the princess. Alone and hungry in the forest, Snow White came across a little cottage which belonged to seven dwarfs. The dwarfs let her stay at their cottage back, and they all lived happily ...

Once upon a time, there was a beautiful castle in a land far far away. In the magnificent castle there lived the most beautiful queen.

To pass the time, the queen used to sit at a window to do some embroidery[1] as a favourite hobby.

On a cold winter day, she was sewing this time and gazing at the snowflakes falling like feathers from the sky and gently depositing on the garden soil forming a huge white and shiny carpet in the sun. Suddenly, she pricked her finger with the needle, and three drops of blood fell onto the snow on the ebony[2] window-frame.

"Oh, I wish I had a baby girl, with a skin as white as snow, and lips as red as blood, and hair as black as the wood of the window-frame, and a heart full of joy and happiness," she said to herself.

[1].**Embroidery** /ɪmˈbrɔɪd(ə)ri/ art of sewing designs on cloth with a needle

[2].**Ebony** /ˈɛbəni/ a very hard dark wood of a tropical tree

Soon after, the queen indeed gave birth to a baby girl with a skin as white as snow, lips as red as blood, and with hair as black as ebony. They named her Snow White.

Everyone was fascinated by the splendid beauty of this child.

The royal couple's joy was indescribable.

Unfortunately, after a few years, the queen fell seriously ill. Despite all the medical care given to her by the greatest doctors in the kingdom, the poor woman finally died. Snow White was just a child then still playing with dolls...

The king sank in great sadness for several weeks. After a year of mourning[1], he had to remarry, both to give a queen to his country and a substitute[2] mother for Snow White.

---

[1].**Mourning** /ˈmɔːnɪŋ/ the expression of sorrow (great sadness) for someone's death

[2].**Substitute** /ˈsʌbstɪtjuːt/ someone or something that takes the

She was a beautiful woman, but proud and haughty[1], and she could not bear that anyone else should surpass her in beauty.

When she was young, a fairy gave her a talking magic mirror.

She often admired herself in the mirror and asked it, "Mirror, mirror, who is the loveliest lady in the land?"

The reply was always; "You are, your Majesty".

Then she was satisfied, because she knew that the looking-glass spoke the truth.

Feeling ever so proud, the queen would kiss the mirror and put it back in its place, singing a merry tune.

Years passed and Snow White grew up to be outstandingly beautiful and was the embodiment of captivating kindness day by day. The queen was so vain[2] and proud of

---

place of another person or thing

[1].**Haughty** /ˈhɔːti/ unfriendly and seeming to consider yourself better than other people

her own beauty that she did not seem to notice Snow White's splendid beauty.

And once when the queen asked her looking-glass, "looking-glass, who in this land is the loveliest of all."

It answered, "You are lovelier than all who are here, lady queen. But more beautiful still is snow-white, as I can see."

Then the queen was shocked, and turned yellow and green with envy.

She put back the mirror in its place with a trembling hand and exclaimed, "How come? I don't believe it! That pretentious little girl, more beautiful than me!"

From that hour, whenever she looked at snow-white, her heart heaved[1] in her breast; she hated the girl so much.

---

[2].**Vain** /veɪn/ excessively proud of or concerned about one's own appearance, qualities, achievements, etc.; conceited

[1].**Heart heaved** moved with some powerful emotion

And envy and pride grew higher and higher in her heart, so that she had no peace day or night. She always repeated, to herself "I don't want to see her anymore! I can't stand her anymore! She must get out of my sight! She must disappear! By any means!"

Finally, she decided to speak to one of the palace huntsmen whom she thought she could trust. ''Take Snow White on the hunt with you," she said to him,

"Once deep in the forest, kill her, and bring me back her heart as proof. She must disappear!"

Of course, he was taken aback[1] but could not argue.

"At your command, your majesty," said the hunter, bowing[2].

---

[1].**Taken aback**: amazed, astonished, astounded, , dumbfounded

[2].**Bow** /bəʊ/ to bend the head or body forward as a way of showing respect

"Cut out her heart and bring it to me so I can be sure you killed her, I promise you a very big reward, I will make you rich until the end of your life."

"I have understood, your majesty, you can rely on me," said the huntsman, bowing a second time.

Then, the queen called Snow White herself and offered to accompany the huntsman. "You need a little fresh air", she said, "Just enjoy the beauty of nature and have fun with butterflies!

Very confident, Snow White left in the company of the huntsman. They arrived in the middle of the forest, and the man did not intend to take action. He felt uncomfortable. Of course, he was used to kill animals every day, but killing a human being, an innocent being, is completely different. He no longer thought of the reward promised by the queen, but only of the horror of the crime he was ordered to commit.

Succumbing to[1] the innocent beauty and the candid kindness of Snow White, the huntsman dropped down on a bended knee and announced to her, "Actually, princess, the queen asked me to bring you here to kill you, I think she is jealous of your beauty..."

Snow White started quivering with fear, then tears came to her eyes and her scarlet lips began to tremble.

"How dare she put me to death because I'm beautiful!" she exclaimed. But she's crazy!"

At that moment, a deer ran past them. With a quick gesture, the huntsman shot it with an arrow that made it fall dead on the spot[2]. He took out his long, sharp knife, opened its chest and pulled out its heart.

---

[1].**Succumb** /səˈkʌm/ to be overcome or overpowered by something; to submit or yield to something

"I will give her this heart instead of yours," he said to the princess, "but you won't be able to return to the palace, because even if I tell the queen everything, she will contradict me and charge[1] me of having kidnapped you, and will have me executed and then look for another way to get rid of[2] you."

"What will become of me then?" said the princess, crying bitterly.

"I will leave you here, and may God help you," he said, "if the queen finds out that I tricked her, I am lost...I have a wife and children, you know..."

Then the huntsman left, leaving Snow White completely hopeless and helpless.

---

[2]. **On the spot** at that moment or place

[1]. **Charge** /tʃɑːdʒ/ to accuse, incriminate

[2]. **Get rid of** to relieve or free oneself of (something or someone unpleasant or undesirable)

But now the poor child was all alone in the great forest, and so terrified that she looked at all the leaves on the trees, and did not know what to do. Then she began to run, and ran over sharp stones and through thorns, and the wild[1] beasts ran past her, but did her no harm.

She thought she could feel terrible eyes spying[2] on her, and she heard strange sounds and rustlings[3] that made her heart thump. At last, overcome by tiredness, she fell asleep curled[4] under a tree.

Snow White slept fitfully[5], wakening from time to time with a start[6] and staring into the darkness round her.

---

[1].**Wild** /waɪld/ Wild animals or plants live or grow in natural surroundings and are not looked after by people

[2].**Spy** (on) /spaɪ/ to watch secretely

[3].**Rustle** v. /ˈrʌs(ə)l/ Rustling: the sound that paper or leaves make when they move

[4].**Curl** /kəːl/ to assume a spiral or curved shape

[5].**Fitfully** /ˈfɪtf(ə)li, ˈfɪtfʊli/ not regularly or continuously; intermittently

[6].**Start** /staːt/ a sudden movement of surprise or alarm

Several times, she thought she felt something, or somebody touch her as she slept.

At last, the forest was stirring[1] to life and you could hear the sound of birds again and the little girl was glad to see how silly her fears had been. However, the thick trees were like a wall round her, and as she tried to find out where she was, she came upon a path.

She walked along it, hopefully. On she walked till she came to a clearing[2].

There stood a strange cottage, with a tiny door, tiny windows and a tiny chimney pot. After some hesitation, she knocked and waited.

---

[1].**Stir** /stɔ:/ to move or cause to move slightly; **stir to life** : to be active or busy

[2].**Clearing** /ˈklɪərɪŋ/ an open space in a forest

Receiving no reply, she pushed the small door open and found herself in a sort of both living and dining room.

"l wonder who lives here?" she said to herself, peeping[1] round the kitchen.

"What tiny plates! And spoons! And glasses of water! There must be seven of them, the table's laid for seven people."

There was food in each of the plates and water in the glasses. Upstairs there was a bedroom with seven neat[2] little beds.

On the whole, it looked like a house, equipped with everything, that had been reduced to a third of its original size by a magic wand[3].

---

[1].**Peep** /piːp/ to look quickly and furtively at something, especially through a narrow opening

[2].**Neat** /niːt/ tidy, with everything in its place

[3].**Magic wand** /ˌmædʒ.ɪk ˈwɒnd/ a short thin stick used for performing magic or magic tricks

As she was starving to death, she began to eat a little out of each plate and drank some water out of each glass.

She then went into a small bedroom where seven small beds were lined up.

As she was so tired, she lay down upon one of the little beds, but none of them fitted her, one was too long, another too short, but at last she put three beds side by side, stretched out on them and quickly fell into a deep sleep.

Towards the end of the afternoon, seven very tiny men returned home.

They were seven dwarfs! Seven people of ridiculously short stature and clownish appearance.

"Someone has come to our place," said one of the dwarfs, the door is open.

'Someone has moved the chairs," said another dwarf.

'Someone's been eating out of my plate, said a third dwarf.

"Someone's been eating out of my plate, too!" the other dwarfs cried together. Nevertheless, they all sat down at a table and ate what remained in their plates and drank what remained in their glasses.

Then they went to their bedroom to spend the night.They were so terribly startled[1] that they nearly collapsed[2] when they discovered Snow White sleeping in their beds.

"Who is it?" said one of the dwarfs.

"What is she doing here?" said another dwarf.

"She has taken our beds," said a third dwarf.

"She is so beautiful, though!" said a fourth dwarf. Very beautiful really!"

---

[1].**Startle** /ˈstɑːt(ə)l/ to cause to feel sudden shock or alarm

[2].**Collapse** /kəˈlaps/ (of a person) fall down and become unconscious

"Don't make any noise," said a
you're going to wake her up.
"Yes, we should let her sleep quie   , said
a sixth dwarf.

They then tiptoed to the dining room and
spent the night there, on makeshift[1] beds,

Snow White did not wake up until the
next morning. It took her a few seconds to
remember where she was.

Hearing some voices nearby, she opened
the bedroom door and was stunned[2] at the
sight of the seven dwarfs bustling[3] around
in the dining room.

They all said 'hello' to her, at the same
time with lisping[4] voices.

---

[1].**Makeshift** /ˈmeɪkʃɪft/ temporary and of low quality, but used
because of a sudden need
[2].**Stunned** /stʌnd/ so shocked that one is temporarily unable to
react; astonished

[3].**Bustle** /ˈbʌs(ə)l/ to move in an energetic and busy manner
[4].**Lisping** mispronunciation of the sounds

ow White stood there staring at them with amazement before answering their greeting. Then she asked them in a surprised voice, "Where am I? Who are you?"

"We are the seven dwarfs," replied the eldest dwarf, and you are here with us, we live in the forest by hunting and eating the fruits that nature provides for us. And you, who are you and what are you doing here?"

Snow White introduced herself and then told them that her step-mother had wished to have her killed, but the huntsman had spared her life, and that she had run for the whole day, until at last she had found their dwelling[1].

On hearing her story, tears sprang to the dwarfs' eyes. Then one of them said, as he noisily blew his nose: "Stay here with us!" "Hooray! Hooray!" they cheered, dancing joyfully round the little girl.

---

[1].**Dwelling** /ˈdwɛlɪŋ/ a house, flat, or other place of residence

Then the eldest dwarf said to her, "Don't worry about your stepmother leaving you in the forest. We love you and we'll take care of you! If you look after our house, cook, make the beds, wash, and if you keep everything tidy and clean you can stay with us and you will want for nothing[1]."

Snow White gratefully accepted their hospitality.

All the dwarfs shouted again for joy, happy to have such a pretty princess at home.

"We're going to leave now," continued the dwarf, "we will cut some wood to make a bed for your size and we will not return until sunset. We will bring back game[2] and fruit."

---

[1].**Want for nothing** to be in no great need of anything; not to lack anything

[2].**Game** /geɪm/ wild animals hunted for food

"I will be looking forward to your return," said Snow White.

The dwarfs knew the girl would be alone the whole day, so they warned her and said, "beware of your step-mother, she will soon know that you are here, be sure to let no one come in."

"Okay," said Snow White.

And she stayed with them. She did the housework for them. In the mornings they went to the mountains and looked for copper and gold, in the evenings they came back, and then their dinner had to be ready.

Everyone in the king's palace wondered where Snow White had gone.

They looked for her everywhere, but in vain. The poor king shed warm tears and the wicked[1] queen wept too, pretending to share her husband's sadness.

But the queen, believing that she had eaten snow-white's heart, could not but think that

---

[1].**Wicked** /wɪkɪd/ evil or morally wrong

she was again the first and most beautiful of all, and she went to her mirror and asked, "Mirror, my beautiful mirror, who in this land is the most beautiful of all?"

And the mirror answered, "Oh, queen, you are the most beautiful of all I see, but over the hills, where the seven dwarfs live, snow-white is still alive and well, and none is so beautiful as she."

But her hopes were dashed[1], because the mirror replied: "The loveliest in the land is still Snow White, who lives in the seven dwarfs' cottage, down in the forest."

The stepmother was beside herself[2] with rage.

---

[1].**Dash someone's hopes** to ruin someone's hopes; to put an end to someone's dreams or aspirations

[2].**Beside oneself** In a state of extreme agitation with worry, grief, or anger

[1].**Damn** /dam/ adj. used to express anger or frustration with someone or something

"She must die! She must die!" she screamed. "The damn[1] huntsman has tricked me, he will pay dear for it!" she said furiously.

A few days later, around mid-afternoon, Snow White was looking through the window enjoying the view of the little multicoloured birds and butterflies fluttering nearby. Suddenly, she saw an old woman approaching with a quiet step.

She was carrying a small canvas bag on her back and several necklaces[2] of flowers hanging from her arm.

"So you live here, in the middle of the forest?" said the old woman to Snow White.

"Yes," replied Snow White in her usual friendly voice.

"And you, where are you going now? Are you on a journey?"

---

[2].**Necklace** /ˈnɛklɪs/ an ornamental chain worn round the neck

"No," replied the old woman, I'm just picking flowers to make necklaces and sell them on the Market Place, in town."

"It's a nice job. Your flowers are very pretty," said Snow White, smiling.

"As you are so beautiful and so nice, I offer you a necklace for nothing," said the old woman.

"Oh, that's very kind of you," said Snow White in a happy voice.

The old woman approached the window sill, chose the most beautiful of her necklaces and put it around Snow White's neck.

The girl thanked the old woman, and then went to look at herself in a small looking-glass hanging on one of the walls of the room. Unfortunately, she was unaware[1] that the old woman was none other than the wicked queen, disguised as a peasant, and

---

[1].**Unaware** /ʌnəˈwɛː/ having no knowledge of a situation or fact

that the necklace of flowers that she had given her was magic.

No sooner had she taken a few steps than she felt suffocated as the necklace had tightened[1] around her neck and prevented her from breathing.

Before she thought of tearing the magic flowers from her neck, she collapsed on the ground, motionless.

When the dwarfs returned at the end of the day, they found Snow White lying still[2] on the ground, apparently lifeless.

"What's the matter with her?" exclaimed one of the dwarfs.

"What's happening to her?" cried out a second dwarf.

"She is dead!" lamented a third dwarf.

"No, she's only passed out," said a fourth dwarf.

---

[1].**Tighten** /ˈtaɪt(ə)n/ to close or fasten something firmly

[2].**Still** motionless

"Look at those flowers around her neck;" noticed a fifth dwarf, "she didn't have them this morning."

One of the dwarfs pulled the necklace and tore it off. Immediately, Snow White opened her eyes and regained consciousness.

"Where am I"? she said, looking with a pale face at the dwarfs around her.

"We found you unconscious on the ground," said one of the dwarfs, "what happened? Where do these flowers come from?"

"Ah, I remember now," said Snow White, "it was a nice old woman who gave me a necklace of pretty flowers."

"It's probably a magic necklace that stifles[1] the wearer," said a second dwarf.

---

[1].**Stifle** /ˈstʌɪf(ə)l/ to make (someone) unable to breathe properly; suffocate

"It must be the wicked queen who sent this old woman to kill you," said a third dwarf.

"But it's horrible!" said Snow White, with tears in her eyes.

"Never open the door again to strangers and accept nothing from anyone," said a fourth dwarf.

"From now on, I will be more careful," promised Snow White.

*   *   *   *

Next morning, believing she got forever rid of Snow White, the wicked queen once again consulted her magic mirror to be sure that she had become again the most beautiful.

"Mirror, my sweet mirror," she said to it, "is there now anyone more beautiful than me in this land?"

To her surprise, the mirror replied, "you are very beautiful, your Majesty, but Snow White is still more beautiful than you."

Beside herself with anger, the wicked queen exclaimed, "Incredible! Is she still alive? the cursed[1] bitch! The damn creature! How did she survive my magic flowers? But I will eventually[2] find a way to get rid of her!"

And when she had at last thought of something to do, she painted her face, and disguised herself like an old peasant woman so that no one could know her.

Then she put a poisoned apple with the others in her basket. Taking the quickest way into forest, she crossed the swamp[3] at the edge of the trees.

She reached the bank[4] unseen, just as Snow White stood was waving goodbye to the seven dwarfs on their way to the mine.

---

[1].**Cursed** /ˈkɔːsɪd,kɔːst/ used to express annoyance or irritation

[2].**Eventually** in the end, finally

[3].**Swamp** /swɒmp/ an area of low-lying, uncultivated ground where water collects

Snow White was in the kitchen when she heard the sound at the door: KNOCK! KNOCK!

"Who's there?" she asked suspiciously[1], remembering the dwarfs' advice.

"I'm an old peasant woman selling apples," came the reply.

"I don't need any apples, thank you," she replied.

"But they are beautiful apples and ever so juicy!" said the soft voice from outside the door.

"I'm not supposed to open the door to anyone," said the little girl, who did not want to disobey her friends.

"And quite right too! Good girl! If you promised not to open up to strangers, then

---

[4].**Bank** the land alongside a river or lake

[1].**Suspiciously** /səˈspɪʃəsli/ feeling doubt or no trust in someone or something

of course you can't buy. You are a good girl indeed!"

Then the old woman went on. "And as a reward for being good, I'm going to make you a gift of one of my apples!"

Without a further thought, Snow White opened the door just a little, to take the apple.

"There! Now isn't that a nice apple?"

Snow White bit into the fruit, and as she did, fell to the ground unconscious: the effect of the terrible poison left her lifeless instantaneously. Now laughing evilly, the wicked stepmother hurried off. But as she ran back across the swamp, she stumbled[1] and fell into the quicksand[2].

---

[1].**Stumble** /ˈstʌmb(ə)l/ trip or momentarily lose one's balance; almost fall

[2].**Quicksand** /ˈkwɪksænd/ deep wet sand that sucks in anyone trying to walk across it

No one heard her cries for help, and she disappeared without a trace.

Meanwhile, the dwarfs came out of the mine to find the sky had grown dark and stormy. Loud thunder echoed through the valleys and streaks of lightning ripped the sky.

Worried about Snow White they ran as quickly as they could down the mountain to the cottage.

There they found Snow White, lying lifeless, the poisoned apple by her side. They did their best to revive her, but it was no use.

They wept and wept for a long time.

"Our poor Snow White is gone! She is dead!"

"The unfortunate girl died because of the jealousy of the wicked queen!"

"Dying so young, what an injustice!"

"She was so pretty and so kind!"

"How are we going to live without her? I always want to gaze at her and admire her!"

"Me too!" cried all the other dwarfs together.

"Don't bury[1] her; we must keep her among us so that she will be one of us!"

"Yes, but how can we do that?"

They all started to think about finding a solution. Suddenly one of them suggested, "What about placing her in the glass box, you know the huge box that we once found in a cave."

"Yes, I quite remember that," said one of the dwarfs, the one we thought was a magic box.

"Good idea," said another dwarf, "Once she is protected by the glass, nothing will happen to her!"

"Yes, she will always keep her white and radiant complexion[2]."

---

[1].**Bury** /ˈberi/ to put a dead body into the ground

"We will place the box under the tree in front of the cottage, so we can admire her everyday, when leaving and returning."

Six of them went out to get the box, while the seventh stayed next to Snow White to watch over her. They were quickly back. They gently stretched Snow White down the bottom of the box and put back the lid[1]. It looked as if the box was designed for her. Then they carried it gently and placed it under the tree on large stones as support. Under the transparency of the glass, Snow White's face looked even more radiant than before.

Everyday, the dwarfs spent some time gazing at her with great affection and love.

---

[2].**Complexion** /kəmˈplek.ʃən/ the natural appearance of the skin on a person's face, especially its colour or quality

[1].**Lid** /lɪd/ a cover on a container, that can be lifted up or removed

Several years passed in this way, without the slightest change in her complexion and the whole appearance of Snow White.

The forest animals had got into the habit of admiring her and frolicking[1] around the glass box.

After some time, the place had become the meeting place for all kinds of animals: butterflies, birds, rabbits, gazelles...

One of the dwarfs had to stay everyday by the box on the look-out to prevent animals from breaking the glass.

Finally, the dwarves no longer needed to go hunting since the prey[2] animals came to them, thanks to Snow White, and they only had to reach out to capture them.

---

[1].**Frolic** /ˈfrɒl.ɪk/ to play and behave in a happy way

[2].**Prey** /preɪ/ animal hunted for food

They then spent all their time near Snow White, whose admiration they shared with all the creatures of the forest.

In the royal palace, the wicked queen kept rejoicing her success and victory.

Some days, she would sometimes ask her magic mirror for fun, "Mirror, my dear mirror, is there anyone more beautiful than me in this land?"

At which, the mirror without fail[1], replied, "Your Majesty, you are always the most beautiful, there is no one that can equal your beauty."

She would then put the mirror back in its place, smiling and feeling quite at ease.

One day, a prince from a neighbouring country came to the forest on a hunting expedition.

By happy coincidence, he passed near the cottage of the seven dwarfs. When he noticed the gathering of many animals, he

[1]. **Without fail** with no exception; always

got closer. He then saw the dwarfs sitting around the glass box in which Snow White looked to be sleeping.

The prince got off his horse to take a closer look. He was dazzled[1] by the divine beauty of Snow White and couldn't help[2] exclaiming, "My God, how beautiful she is! I have never seen such splendour in my entire life!"

"You are right, your Highness," said one of the dwarfs, unfortunately, she is dead and we keep her in this state thanks to this glass box which is magic."

"Dead! Incredible!" exclaimed the prince. But she is sleeping peacefully!"

So the dwarfs told him Snow White's story and all that the wicked queen, her stepmother, had done to her.

---

[1].**Dazzled** /ˈdaz(ə)ld/ extremely impressed

[2].**Can't help** not to be able to control or stop something

The prince could not hold back the tears of sadness and sympathy. Without stopping to look at Snow White, he said, "I want to touch her one last time and give her a goodbye kiss."

The dwarfs helped him raise the lid and he began to gently cuddle[1] Snow White's soft face.

To his surprise, he found that her cheeks were warm, not cold and stiff[2] as he expected.

"She's alive! She is breathing!" he said in a trembling voice.

The seven dwarfs were thunderstruck[3], and remained speechless.

"She is alive, I'm telling you!" repeated the prince. "Her skin is warm and not cold like that of a dead person!"

---

[1].**Cuddle** to hold close in an affectionate manner; hug tenderly

[2].**Stiff** hard

[3].**Thunderstruck** /ˈθʌndəstrʌk/ extremely surprised or shocked

"Impossible!" said one of the dwarfs, "she's been lying in this box for a few years."

"Yes, she's never moved," added another dwarf.

Without listening to them, the prince began to feel her cheeks, her mouth and throat in an excited manner. He parted her lips and noticed something between her teeth. So he opened her mouth and removed the piece of apple which was stuck there.

Immediately, Snow White sighed[1] and blinked[2].

"Oh, heavens, where am I?" she cried while looking at the prince and the seven dwarfs leaning over her, with eyes wide-open.

---

[1].**Sigh** /saɪ/ emit a long, deep audible breath

[2].**Blink** /blɪŋk/ to shut and open the eyes quickly

"She's alive! She's speaking! Snow White is alive! Hooray!" cried out the seven dwarfs together.

They began to jump for joy, clap[1] and shout. As for the prince, he could not hold back tears of emotion.

He helped Snow White rise and get out of the glass box, and then all of them went into the cottage.

The dwarfs told Snow White how they found her lifeless, and then laid her in the glass box and the prince told her how he brought her back to life. In turn, Snow White told them how an old woman had given her half an apple.

"I just remember biting into the apple," she said, "then nothing! Now, I feel as if I have slept very long and I'm hungry like the wolf.

---

[1].**Clap** /klæp/ strike the palms of (one's hands) together repeatedly

The dwarfs prepared a copious meal. They had dinner then, no one wanted to go to bed, and they stayed up very late in the evening.

The prince said to Snow White

"I love you more than everything in the world, come with me to my father's palace, you will be my wife."

He then added, smiling "but promise me that you will no longer be approached by any old woman but my mother."

"I promise," said Snow White smiling, "but I'm always thinking of my father."

"I will invite him myself to our wedding," said the prince and I will tell him the whole truth, so your wicked stepmother will be punished for her misdeeds[1]."

The next morning, they headed for the prince's kingdom.

---

[1].**Misdeed** /ˌmɪsˈdiːd/ an act that is criminal or bad

At the same time, in Snow White's father's palace, the wicked queen had, by chance, decided to consult her magic mirror again.

"Mirror, my sweet mirror," she said, "is there anyone more beautiful than me in this land?"

"You're always very beautiful, Your Majesty," replied the mirror, but Snow White is still more beautiful than you."

"How?" she cried out, "she's still alive after all these years!"

Unable to contain her anger, the wicked queen threw the mirror on the ground with all her might[1].

The ice shattered and scattered in all directions. By a strange coincidence, a long and pointed piece of glass sank deep into her heart, and she dropped dead on the spot.

---

[1].**Might** n. force

In the other palace, the prince, Snow White and the seven dwarfs were welcomed with great ceremony.

After seeing Snow White and hearing all her story, the king ordered that preparations for the wedding should begin immediately.

As promised, the prince left for Snow White's father's palace to invite him to the wedding. He was accompanied by a few lords and two of the dwarfs.

When they arrived, they found the palace plunged in sadness. The prince introduced himself and told Snow White's father about everything.

When he had finished, the king said to him, "God punished her for her wickedness; she died yesterday after she accidentally pierced her heart by a piece of glass from her magic mirror and we're going to bury her, but it is a day of misfortune that turns into a day of happiness for me!"

He then hugged the prince, kissed him and added, "Let's leave now, I'm looking forward to seeing Snow White again, but I want you to come and live here after the wedding, I will leave my throne for you."

"It's my great honour, your Majesty," said the prince, bowing.

A few hours later, Snow White threw herself with great emotion into her father's arms and burst out crying.

The joy of being together again was indescribable. Everyone was happy and no one regretted the death of the wicked queen, who had met the end she deserved.

Printed in Great Britain
by Amazon

18912085R00031